FOR LARA, ALWAYS - AW

FOR ABIGAIL & JACOB - DB

LITTLE TIGER PRESS LTD,
an imprint of the Little Tiger Group
1 Coda Studios, 189 Munster Road,
London SW6 6AW
Imported into the EEA by Penguin Random House
Ireland, Morrison Chambers, 32 Nassau Street,
Dublin D02 YH68
www.littletiger.co.uk

First published in Great Britain 2022

A CIP catalogue record for this book is available from the British Library

All rights reserved • ISBN 978-1-80104-287-1

Printed in China • LTP/2800/4392/0122

1 3 5 7 9 10 8 6 4 2

AGENT LLAMA

ALPACA ATTACK!

ANGELA WOOLFE   DUNCAN BEEDIE

LONDON

An empty lab, the dead of night.
A **figure** lowers from a height.

Who's this llama dropping by?

It's **CHARLIE PALMER**,

super-spy!

A TWIST, A ROLL, A DOUBLE FLIP!

She's here to find a microchip.

On it, plans for P-19,
An evil Pasta-Splat Machine!

Clever Charlie
grabs the tech . . .

She heads home,
then makes
a check:

"It's wiped!
Those plans have GONE!!"

There's something
fishy going on . . .

She calls HQ – but no reply.
"That's very strange . . . I wonder why . . ."

Then
BREAKING NEWS
is on her screen . . .

"Live reporting from the scene
In Dublin, Delhi, Delaware –
SPAGHETTI'S landing everywhere!

We've shut the schools!
We're climbing trees!

The streets are full of sprinkled CHEESE!
The waves of sauce are getting grim:

We fear for those who cannot swim!

And who's behind this pasta drama?"

CHARLIE does a double-take:
"That isn't me! It's just a fake!
And who fires pasta from a drone?!
I have to stop this evil clone."

She grabs some gadgets from the store
She keeps concealed beneath the floor:

A teddy with a **_LASER EYE;_**

A **_SURFBOARD_** in an apple pie;

Banana primed with Supa-Slip
And helicopter-paperclip.

Then revs her turbo engine . . . **_VROOOOOOM!_**
She's off to stop the pasta doom!

The latest Pasta-Splat report
Is coming from a beach resort
Where tangled tourists, stressed and sweaty,
Wrestle with *EXTREME SPAGHETTI!*

Our hero Charlie's on the case!
Not an eyelash out of place,

PALMER

searches for the meanie,

Fancy in her gold bikini.

Look! What's that? A distant yacht . . .

She dodges pasta (ouch, that's hot!)
And revs her engine, gaining speed.

She's going very fast indeed . . .

Her apple pie becomes a board
(A couple of the sharks applaud).

She surfs towards a looming lair.
"The pasta villain must be there!"

And now, outside, she's rising high –
Sixty storeys in the sky –
To reach the Pasta-Splat Machine . . .

It's just a **keyboard** and a screen!

A figure turns . . . oh, this is trouble:

CHARLIE'S looking at . . . HER DOUB

"Palmer – what a nice surprise.
I'll just remove this fab disguise!"
So who's the Pasta-Splat attacker?

**ROGUE ALPACA –
HARLEY HACKER!**

Charlie gasps. "Hey, I know you!
You used to be an agent too!"
But Hacker sneers, "That all went wrong
When perfect Palmer came along.

Your super skills
put me to shame.
For what comes next,
you'll take the blame!
Those pasta-splats were just for fun.
My final target is . . .

THE SUN!"

Then, in a flash,
she disappears!
And look – confirming
Charlie's fears –

Are off to make the **sun explode!**
They're passing Venus, gaining speed –
It's looking very bad indeed . . .

The drones explode –
their day is done!
The password worked.
She's saved the sun.

But Harley Hacker's
still a threat!
"My mission isn't
over yet . . ."

So Charlie, swift and sure of hoof,
Starts chasing her across the roof.

The villain fires –
OUR HERO'S ready:
"Thanks a million, LASER Teddy!"

INCOMING CALL: HQ

We never fell for that at ALL!
But once again, you've saved the day!
(We're really sorry, by the way.)

Charlie's chopper starts to soar
Towards a peaceful, sandy shore –
A llama-friendly little nook
For lemon fizz and thrilling book.

We'll leave her there –
on one condition:

WE TAG ALONG ON
HER NEXT MISSION!